MAGICAL TALES

FROM

Fairyland

Woodland Fairies

The Magic Sceptre

MAGICAL TALES

FROM

Fairyland

Woodland Fairies
The Magic Sceptre

Ines Holmes

First published in the UK in 2024 by the Independent Publishing
Network

First edition

Author: Ines Holmes
Email: ines.holmes@icloud.com
Website: www.inesholmes.com
Please direct all enquiries to the author.

ISBN: 978-1-7398003-2-1

Written and illustrated by Ines Holmes

For P.C.H.

CONTENTS

GOBLIN FLAME

"Firth! Hey, Firth!"

Ardeen zoomed through the undergrowth of the Ancient Forest in search of his best friend.

"Over here!" came the response from inside a hollow tree trunk.

"What are you doing in there? I thought you were helping Bluebell collect blackberries?" asked Ardeen as he landed gently on the moss-overgrown trunk.

"I was, but then I found a bee stuck in the spiderwebs in here and helped it escape. Aren't you supposed to study?" asked Firth in return, fluttering up to greet Ardeen.

"Yes, that's what I did when I found this amazing spell turning the leaves of a cercis into a flame that gives off heat, but doesn't scorch anything. Do you want to help me try it out?"

Ardeen unrolled a leaf scroll. Written on it, in the symbols of the Woodland Fairies, was a spell and description of how to use it.

"What does it say?" asked Firth, leaning over

the scroll with what looked like swirls and spider legs to him. He had never learned to read or write the ancient language of the Woodland Fairies. His passion was to look after the animals of the forest, especially any injured creatures. He could talk to any woodland creature in their own language and, like all Woodland Fairies, he could communicate with the trees. Ardeen, on the other hand, was apprentice to Ealdwode, the oldest and wisest Woodland Fairy, keeper of all Woodland Fairy lore and wisdom, and current guardian of the Magic Sceptre. Ardeen studied the hundreds of scrolls that were kept in the old oak tree in the centre of the Ancient Forest, and some day, when Ealdwode's century of guardianship will have come to a close, he will take over his responsibilities.

"We'll need a yellow or red leaf of a cercis, some goblin gold moss and the Magic Sceptre, of course," explained Ardeen as he was deciphering the scroll.

"I know a cave where we can find the goblin gold, but the trees are still pretty green," Firth pointed out.

"I'm sure it will be fine if they haven't changed entirely yet. Let's go, I'm so excited to try this one."

Together they flew to a damp cave with a spring. The two Woodland Fairies blended in perfectly with their surroundings. Their skin colour changed with the

seasons of the woods and was currently a pale green with hints of red, yellow and brown. Their clothes were made from moss and leaves. Their wings were leaf-shaped, and their flying pattern looked just like falling leaves dancing in the wind.

They stepped into the cave which was overgrown with the bio-luminescent moss the Woodland Fairies call goblin gold.

"It's like stepping into another world, isn't it," marvelled Firth, as they walked into the dark cavern, only dimly illuminated by the greenish glow of the moss. Ardeen picked a handful of it.

"Next stop, cercis leaf," he said.

The beautiful, old cercis stood near a warm and sunny clearing in the forest. Ardeen and Firth flew all around the tree, but could indeed not find a single leaf that was fully dressed in autumn colours yet.

"Looks like it's too early in the season for magic fires," said Firth.

"I don't think it matters that much if the leaf is still a little bit green. Let's just use this one, it's nearly all yellow," persisted Ardeen.

"Are you sure? Remember what happened last time when you thought it was okay to use red currant when we couldn't find any black currant?" Firth reminded his sometimes overly keen friend.

"I know, I know, but this is the right leaf. It just

has a bit of green in it," Ardeen assured him. "Let's fly to the Old Oak and get the Magic Sceptre."

"Alright, if you're sure," answered Firth, not sounding very confident at all. Ardeen was his best friend and a very eager student, but he did have a tendency to get overexcited, which made him a rather impatient fairy. However, most of the ancient spells of the Woodland Fairies were very specific when it came to ingredients to be used, and sometimes even time when certain spells could or should be performed. Nevertheless, he followed Ardeen to the Old Oak. It was always exciting to step inside and see it filled with scroll upon scroll. There were shelves overflowing with containers and jars filled with a wide array of pollen dust, preserved flowers, roots and leaves, nuts and seeds, and even mist. Some containers were glowing, while others had strange looking liquids in them. Firth never dared to touch anything, but Ardeen felt quite at home, whizzing around, arranging everything to try out his latest discovery. Ardeen loved to rummage through the old scrolls trying to find a new fun spell to try.

"There, all set up," Ardeen said as he put the Magic Sceptre on the table together with the leaf and moss. The Magic Sceptre was made from the twigs of the Magic Rowan Tree in the far north of the Ancient Forest. The twigs where delicately intertwined,

cradling a red gemstone that glowed like red-hot coal. While all Woodland Fairies have their own magical gifts, it is their Magic Sceptre that is the source of all their magic. Without it, they would not be able to perform any magic spells, which were first and foremost healing spells, and would lead to the loss of their own powers over time if it were to be destroyed or lost.

"Where's Ealdwode?" asked Firth, still a bit unsure about their experiment.

"He's out gathering foxglove pollen. Our stocks are running low and he wanted to have enough to see us through winter."

Ardeen unrolled the scroll and weighed down the ends with small pebbles. Then he formed the cercis leaf into a bowl with his hands, put the goblin gold moss in the middle and, holding the Magic Sceptre above it, read the magic words on the scroll:

"Goblin fire, keep us warm,
light a fire, without harm.
Our dwelling keep warm from the cold,
and let non-scorching flames unfold."

As Ardeen spoke the words, the glow of the luminous moss brightened and intensified, and suddenly burst out into a bright green flame. Both fairy boys marvelled at the beautiful spectre. They touched the flame and felt its warmth, but it didn't burn them. Ardeen was about to exclaim in triumph, when the flame quickly turned to thick smoke, filling the Old Oak library almost instantaneously. Coughing and groping around with their hands to feel their way out of the Old Oak, Ardeen and Firth suddenly bumped into Ealdwode.

"What in the name of the Magic Rowan Tree has happened here?" he exclaimed. He found the Magic Sceptre lying on the table, and with a swift movement of the sceptre, it started to suck in the smoke like a vacuum cleaner. When the smoke was gone, Ealdwode noticed the other ingredients on the table.

"Ah, I see you tried to make a Goblin Flame. I assume the leaf you used had not entirely changed its colour yet?" he said to Ardeen with a raised eyebrow. Ardeen hung his head.

"No, it hadn't," he mumbled. "I thought it would be yellow enough. I'm sorry, Ealdwode. I'm glad you came back when you did."

"No harm done, my boy. I like your eagerness to try our spells, but you need to learn that these instructions are so specific for a reason. There is a right time for everything, and this wasn't the right time for a Goblin Flame. Now, shall we get back to work?" Ealdwode explained, putting his arm around Ardeen's shoulder.

"I'd better be off now," said Firth. "Bluebell will be waiting for me." He was glad to leave the Old Oak again. The incident with the smoke had given him quite a fright, and he was glad Ealdwode had been able to react so quickly. Sometimes he wondered whether it was wise of him to help Ardeen with his experiments when he felt they were not going to work. But there was no stopping him anyway, and he'd rather be there to protect his friend if he could.

Ealdwode and Ardeen spend the rest of the day going through a great variety of healing spells. Ealdwode made him learn them off by heart, focussing particularly on exact timings and amounts. There were spells to heal cuts, stings and broken bones, spells to heal stomach ache and even poisoning from foods and flowers. Ardeen's head was spinning by the end of the day.

"I think you'll have enough to study while I'm away for the next three days visiting my brother in the Southern Forest. I'll leave the Magic Sceptre in your care, but be mindful only to use it in an emergency. No experiments while I'm away, please!" said Ealdwode looking stern. He trusted his studious apprentice, though his excitement often got the better of him.

"I promise, Ealdwode. I won't let you down," Ardeen responded sincerely. He wouldn't admit it, but he was still shaken from the events earlier today and vowed to himself to be more cautious. They said their farewells and Ealdwode set off on his journey.

BAD NEWS

Ardeen spent the next day repeating the healing spells from the previous day and then helped Firth brush the teeth of a particularly cheeky stoat that had managed to get some eggshell stuck in its gums. Later, he flew back to his family's dwelling in the knotty branches of a beech tree. Their home looked like a huge pine cone turned upside down. It was woven from twigs and insulated with moss, fur and feathers they had gathered in the woods. There was a small opening for an entrance at the bottom to keep the warmth in. Dried woodland flowers decorated the inside of the walls, and three hammocks, woven from strips of grass and leaves, hung from the ceiling at different heights — one large one for his parents, and the other two for his sister, Pherenice, and himself.

Ardeen knew something was wrong as soon as he entered. Both his father, Sylvan, and his sister were bent over his parent's hammock, looking very concerned. His mother, Nemorosa, was lying in the hammock and looked very unwell. She was sweating

and shivering at the same time, and her skin looked ashen.

"Mother! What has happened?" exlaimed Ardeen as he flew up to the hammock to join the others.

"Ardeen! Good that you're here," whispered his father, waving him up to join them. "Your mother is resting at the moment. She was helping a badger with a sore paw. When she put belladonna juice on the wound it must have stung quite a bit, because he lashed out and she got scratched. But the really bad thing is that she spilled the entire belladonna juice all over herself and her wound."

Ardeen gasped. Small amounts of belladonna juice were safe to use to clean wounds of injured animals, but any amount ingested by a fairy was absolutely poisonous. The poison had entered his mother's bloodstream through her wound, which in itself would have been easy to heal. But the poison was now pumping through his mother's body, leaving her weak and in pain.

"I'll get Ealdwode," he exclaimed, but then remembered that Ealdwode was away.

"Don't worry, I'll find the right healing spell myself," he reassured his father and flew off to the Old Oak as fast as he could. Panic and worry sped him on. He looked through all healing spells dealing with poisoning he could find. But they were all about other kinds of poisoning, such as accidentally eating a false morel instead of a real one, or getting poisoned by a nettle leaf. Nothing about belladonna poisoning at all. He spent all night looking through scroll after scroll until, finally, buried underneath a big pile of scrolls with weather spells, he found an old scroll with a label that said 'Belladonna Poisoning, DANGEROUS'.

Excited to have finally found the cure, Ardeen began to decipher the script, which proved to be very difficult, as the scroll was fragile and torn in places. He spent hours trying to read it and his eyes started to burn with tiredness. The spell was very complicated and he would require Ealdwode's help to perform it accurately, but Ealdwode would not return before the following evening. Ardeen's heart sank as he continued to read the instructions stating clearly and firmly that the spell had to be performed when a full moon was at its highest point. Otherwise, even the magic of the sceptre would not suffice to heal the poisoning. The next full moon was SIX nights from now. Would his mother last that long? He could do nothing about this without Ealdwode's advice. But, he could at least brew his mother a potion to ease her pain. It was nearly evening again when Ardeen finally returned home, potion in hand.

"Ardeen, where have you been?" asked his

father. "I was getting worried about you. Your mother is getting worse. Have you been able to find a cure?"

Ardeen hung his head.

"I have, but it's a very old and difficult spell. I can't do it without Ealdwode, but he doesn't return until tomorrow. Also, it has to be performed during a full moon, which is another six nights from now. All I could bring her is this potion against the pain. I'm sorry, Father!"

"You've done well, Ardeen. Thank you for the potion. I'll give it to your mother straight away. Now, get some rest. You must be exhausted. There's nothing more we can do at the moment."

Ardeen withdrew to his hammock. He felt very tired and his eyes were burning from reading all the scrolls, but even more than that, he felt frustrated and angry. What good was it to learn all these spells, when he couldn't even help his own mother? Ealdwode's words rang in his ears… 'There's a right time for everything'.

That might be right, Ardeen thought to himself, but what if the right timing for the spell meant, that it would be too late for his mother? Surely the timing had to be right for the patient, too?

With thoughts like this flooding his mind, he eventually dozed off, just to wake up a couple of hours later, still tired, but unable to rest any longer. He flew up to his parent's hammock, where he found his father watching over his mother, gently cooling her head.

"Can't sleep?" asked Sylvan, who looked rather tired himself.

"No, I have too much on my mind. Would you like to get a few hours' rest in my hammock, while I watch over mother?"

"That's very kind of you, Ardeen. I could use a few hours of sleep. Your mother seems to feel much better after taking your potion. Thank you."

Sylvan settled down in Ardeen's hammock and closed his eyes, while Ardeen continued to sponge his mother's forehead. She looked pale and weak, unlike her usual strong and lively self. He would never have imagined that anything could dampen his mother's mood or spirit, and it bothered him a lot to see her like this. Their immortality had suddenly become very fragile.

Nemorosa slowly opened her eyes.

"Have I woken you, Mother?" asked Ardeen anxiously.

"My dear boy, I'm so glad to see you," Nemorosa responded in a faint whisper. "Thank you so much for the potion. I feel much better now."

"But it won't heal you," responded Ardeen hanging his head.

"I know. You've done everything you could."

"But I should be able to do more!" he said hotly.

"You are afraid it will be too late to perform the healing spell," said Nemorosa calmly. "Trust in our magic. Believe that everything will be right in the end, whatever the outcome."

"How can you say that, Mother?" Ardeen exclaimed.

"Because I am not afraid of what lies beyond our realm, my child, and I firmly believe that all is how it is meant to be." She took Ardeen's hand and squeezed it gently. Then she closed her eyes again and whispered with a faint smile "Trust, and don't be afraid."

Ardeen stayed with his mother for the rest of the night. Early the next morning he rushed back to the Old Oak to brew a fresh batch of potion. All the while, he was looking towards the entrance, hoping for Ealdwode to return. He looked up eagerly when he heard a noise, but it was only Firth coming to pay him a visit.

"Oh, it's you," said Ardeen, visibly disappointed.

"What a warm welcome," Firth responded jokingly, but quickly changed his tone when he saw Ardeen's face. "What has happened, Ardeen? You look terrible!"

"I'm sorry, Firth. I was hoping you would be Ealdwode. It's my mother." Ardeen told Firth everything that had occurred since they had last seen each other.

"That's terrible, Ardeen. I am so sorry," said Firth, when Ardeen had finished. "Is there anything I can do to help?"

"I'm afraid not, but please send Ealdwode to our house should you see him before I do."

"Of course, I will."

Firth sat silently watching Ardeen prepare the potion. Neither of them said anything, but Ardeen felt comforted by his best friend's presence, and Firth felt Ardeen needed him, even though he couldn't do much to help. When the potion was finished and Ealdwode still hadn't returned, Ardeen flew back home and Firth set off looking for their healer fairy.

EALDWODE RETURNS

Ardeen was getting more and more impatient. It was nearly night now and Ealdwode still hadn't returned. He had flown back to the Old Oak repeatedly to see if he was there, but there was no sign of him. The potion seemed to soften the symptoms and, all things considered, his mother was fairly comfortable. Deep insight Ardeen knew that Ealdwode would not be able to do more than that until the full moon, but having him back would make him feel much more confident about his mother's recovery. Ealdwode was always calm and reassuring, no matter how serious a situation was.

In the meantime, Firth had not been idle either. Since he had left the Old Oak, he had been looking for Ealdwode, asking everyone else if they had seen him along the way. He went to Ealdwode's dwelling, back to the Old Oak — somehow always missing Ardeen — and down some popular fairy paths towards the Southern Forest, which Ealdwode might choose to return. Just as he was about to give up as daylight was fading fast, he saw Ealdwode approaching. He rushed towards him.

"Ealdwode, Ealdwode, I'm so glad I've finally found you. Something terrible has happened."

"What is it, Firth? Is Ardeen alright?"

Firth retold in a few words what had happened and together they flew to Ardeen's home.

"This is serious. This is serious, indeed," sighed Ealdwode when he had examined Nemorosa. "The poison is attacking her body. Can you see this blue line emerging from her wound? If that reaches her heart, there's nothing more I can do for her."

Sylvan and Ardeen looked gravely at each other. Poor Pherenice tried to put on a brave face, but her eyes filled with tears. She had been helping out as much as she could, getting fresh water and gathering food.

"I know this is very upsetting for you all, but there's not much I can do for her right now," Ealdwode explained in a calm voice. "I believe you have found the spell, Ardeen?"

"Yes, I have. But the scroll says the spell has to be performed in the light of a full moon!" answered Ardeen. "That is still four nights from now. Is there nothing else we can do to help her?"

"Belladonna juice is a very powerful poison and has to be treated with a powerful spell. The Magic Sceptre needs the light of the full moon to enhance its magical powers. Without it, the sceptre on its own will not be strong enough to heal Nemorosa, and could have even worse consequences. The next full moon will be a Magna Luna, which will intensify the spell further, healing Nemorosa entirely. Luckily, there are only a few more days to go. Nemorosa is strong, both in body and in spirit."

"Then we trust everything will be alright," said Sylvan, giving Pherenice an encouraging hug.

"I'll prepare an even stronger potion against the pain and fever for her. Will you help me, Ardeen?"

"Of course," responded Ardeen.

Back at the Old Oak, Ardeen gathered ingredients for the new potion. Ealdwode observed him for a while.

"Ardeen, I can see that you're very upset and that's okay," he began. "We Woodland Fairies believe that everything that happens to us, the good things and the bad, happen for a reason. No matter what the outcome, that is how it's meant be, and we trust that everything will be alright in the end."

"That's what mother has said to me as well, but it's just not fair. Why am I learning everything about

Woodland Fairy magic and healing, when I can't do anything when it matters most?" responded Ardeen, still frustrated with his helplessness. "The moon is nearly full. Surely there's enough moonlight to power the sceptre?"

"No, Ardeen. You mustn't even consider that. Have I not told you enough about the importance of accuracy and timing when it comes to our spells? This is a very powerful spell and it can go seriously wrong if not performed correctly. Be patient and trust in our magic!"

It was nearly midnight, when the new potion was finally finished. Ardeen took it to his mother, but she had taken a turn for the worse in the meantime.

She can't go on like this for another four days, he thought. There must be another way.

PATIENCE ENDS

All day long Ardeen watched his mother getting worse and worse. Finally, he couldn't take it any longer and left to find Firth.

"I'm going to do it tonight, Firth," he told him once he had found him.

"What?" asked Firth in surprise.

"The ritual, I'm going to perform it tonight. I have studied the spell over and over again. I know every detail off by heart."

"But Ardeen, Ealdwode said it needs a full moon to work, it even says so on the scroll, you told me so yourself, and that is still three nights away!" warned Firth.

"I know, I know, but I can't stand by any longer as my mother gets weaker and weaker. The blue line is getting so close to her heart and I don't know if she can wait this long. Maybe it will at least slow down the process, and then we repeat the spell in three days. And anyway, it's a Magna Luna, which makes the light tonight much stronger than it would be during a normal full moon. Maybe it will be enough."

"I'm really not sure, Ardeen. What if it goes wrong? This is such a powerful spell, you don't know what's going to happen."

"I have to try at least. Will you help me? Please, Firth." Ardeen looked pleadingly at his friend. Firth gave a sigh.

"Of course, I'm going to help you. But promise me to be careful."

"I promise."

"Well, what can I do?"

"We have to pick up a few supplies from the Old Oak, including the scroll and the Magic Sceptre. Ealdwode is there at the moment, so we'll have to wait until he flies home tonight, otherwise he'll notice that the scroll and the sceptre are missing."

"Are you really sure about this, Ardeen? I don't like going behind Ealdwode's back like this."

"I don't either, but if he won't do anything to help my mother, I will."

Firth knew that he wouldn't be able to stop Ardeen, and even though he felt more unsure about helping him than ever, he also knew that Ardeen needed him more than ever before. They agreed to meet again after dark, which would still give them enough time to prepare everything before the moon would be at it's highest point, though still three nights away from a full moon.

Ardeen and Firth were rushing around the Old Oak looking for ingredients and arranging them on a large piece of bark that served as a table. Then they set to work. All ingredients had to be crushed and ground to a fine powder. It took a lot of elbow grease, but at last it was done. Then they had to be weighted carefully and mixed in a specific order. The damaged condition of the scroll made the process difficult and slow. Ardeen really wished Ealdwode was there to help him.

Firth noticed a strange buzzing sound in the usually calm and peaceful Old Oak, as if it was trying to warn them. A bad feeling overcame him, but Ardeen was too focussed on the spell to notice anything else around him.

Once it was finally done, they bundled the powder up in a leaf and flew to Ardeen's home. They hid the bundle outside before entering, as Ardeen didn't want his father to see it. Sylvan had fallen asleep with Nemorosa gently wrapped in his arms. Days of sleeplessness had taken their toll.

"There's no way of getting my father out of the hammock," Ardeen whispered to Firth. "I'll have to perform the spell like this."

"I'll get the bundle," replied Firth.

Ardeen unrolled the scroll and carefully (and very quietly) mixed the powder with a small amount of clean water to make a paste.

"Now for the difficult part," whispered Ardeen. "I have to charge the sceptre with moonlight. Then you'll have to apply this paste to my mother's wound as I say the spell. I hope it doesn't wake her up. It won't work if she wipes it off before the spell has been completed."

"And you are really sure you want to take the risk, Ardeen?" asked Firth for the last time, already guessing the answer.

"I have to, she's my mother," said Ardeen.

Ardeen picked up the sceptre and the scroll, while Firth took the small bowl with the pasty mix of ingredients. They fluttered up to the hammock as silently as possible. Ardeen looked out of a small window to check the moon was at its highest point now, then he held the sceptre straight into a moonbeam for a few minutes.

"I hope that's enough," he whispered.

He lowered the sceptre over Nemorosa's body and gave Firth a nod to apply the paste, while repeatedly whispering the spell under his breath.

The red gemstone in the sceptre began to glow. Wisps of smoke rose from the wound as if the belladonna juice was evaporating from it. The blue line became shorter and paler.

"It's working!" said Ardeen, still whispering, but barely able to contain his joy.

But the Magic Sceptre continued to glow brighter and brighter.

"Ardeen!" exclaimed Firth. "I think the sceptre is about to burst into flames!"

At that moment, Sylvan and Nemorosa woke up.

"Ardeen, what's going on?" asked his father.

The sceptre began to feel hot in Ardeen's hands, but he didn't dare drop it. Then he felt the twigs of the Magic Rowan Tree, which held the gemstone in the sceptre, begin to split and break, until the sceptre fell apart. All that was left of the sceptre was the red gemstone, which Ardeen had caught in his hands. It had lost its mystical red glow, and looked dull and dark.

Everyone was in shock. Pherenice, who had also been woken up by the noises, fluttered up to them.

"What has happened?"

Everyone looked at Ardeen.

"I…I was trying to heal mother," he stuttered.

"Ardeen," said his mother weakly "You have been so worried about me. You tried the spell even though you knew it wasn't the right time!"

"I couldn't bear to see you suffer like this any longer. And it was working…"

Nemorosa looked down at her injured arm. The blue line had indeed faded a little and the wound looked better, but without the Magic Sceptre they wouldn't be able to heal her entirely now.

"Firth," said Sylvan quietly. "Please get Ealdwode, immediately."

"Firth flew off as fast as he could. His head was spinning. What had just happened? The Magic Sceptre was destroyed! When he reached Ealdwode's dwelling, he wasn't able to explain anything. He just tugged his arm and said:

"Come quickly."

Ealdwode was confused, but followed Firth. When they arrived at Ardeen's home, they found him sitting on the edge of the hammock, staring at the gemstone in his hands.

"What have I done," he repeated over and over again, shaking his head.

"Ardeen," said Ealdwode calmly but firmly. "You were told not to try the spell before the moon was full. Not only is the sceptre destroyed, which means we can't heal your mother, but you've put all of us in grave danger. You know our magic powers are connected to the sceptre. Without it, they will fade and leave us defenceless."

Ardeen hung his head. This had not been part of the plan.

"Nevertheless," continued Ealdwode. "Not all is lost."

Ardeen looked up at him with a questioning look.

"Provided you are willing to make amends, that is."

"Of course I am. Whatever it takes," responded Ardeen within the blink of an eye. "What can I do?"

"We need to make a new sceptre, and to do so, we need new branches from the Magic Rowan Tree. But beware, you must follow my instructions to the letter to select the right branches," warned Ealdwode.

"I will, I promise. But how will I find the Magic Rowan Tree?" Ardeen asked.

"I can help with that," said Firth. "I can speak to the animals. They will help us find it."

"I can't ask you to come with me, Firth. I've asked too much of you as it is," said Ardeen.

"You didn't ask, I offered. I helped you cause this, and I'll help you make amends." This time, Firth was finally confident he was doing the right thing.

Ealdwode described in great detail which kinds of twigs and branches they would require to make a new Magic Sceptre. They had to have a certain length and thickness. They needed to be flexible, but not too young, and many other qualities. This time, Ardeen listened with great care, determined to get it right.

"You'll have to set off with the first morning light," finished Ealdwode.

Sylvan and Nemorosa had been listening silently, but now Sylvan raised his concerns.

"Are you sure it will be wise for Ardeen to undertake this journey? He hasn't slept properly in days, and the Northern Forest is not without danger! Why don't I go?"

"I understand your concern, Sylvan, but I'm afraid that won't be possible. The magic gemstone has its own memory. Only the hand that damaged or destroyed the sceptre can use the gemstone to make a

new one. It has to be Ardeen."

"I'll be careful, I promise," Ardeen said to his parents, and turning to Ealdwode "I won't disappoint you again."

THE NORTHERN FOREST

Ardeen and Firth set off at first light. The weather was pleasant enough for the journey, but Ardeen felt the strain of the last few days. All that was urging him on, was his desire to help his mother and to make amends.

Firth watched his friend carefully and realised that they wouldn't make it to the Magic Rowan Tree like this. Determined or not, Ardeen wouldn't be able to keep this up much longer. Around midday, he suggested a break.

"You know, we could ask the birds for help," he offered.

"Do you think they would help us?" asked Ardeen.

"Let's find out," responded Firth and fluttered away to speak to two robins perched on a branch above them. He soon returned.

"They said they'll carry us until sunset. It's not safe for them to be out after dark."

"That's fantastic," exclaimed Ardeen.

So they set off again. This time, each of them was comfortably seated between the wings of a robin. The flight pattern of a robin is very different to that of a Woodland Fairy, which didn't necessarily make the journey easier, but definitely much faster. The robins flew tirelessly, but sunset came all too soon. Firth thanked them in their own language and then turned to Ardeen.

"What are we going to do now?"

"Let's ask the trees."

Ardeen made himself comfortable in a forked branch and closed his eyes. Though Woodland Fairies can indeed communicate with the trees, they can only do so, when they are completely calm and focussed. Trees are gentle, wise beings and their voices are very faint. They are also quite selective in who they are willing to talk to. Just because a fairy can talk to them, does not mean they are willing to respond. Firth waited patiently, while Ardeen connected with the trees around them. Sometimes, this could take some time. Time, they didn't have. Finally, he opened his eyes again.

"The trees have responded and said the Magic Rowan Tree is still a long way up north. We won't make it there in time on our own. Do you think one of the night animals would help us?" asked Ardeen. "It's not safe for us either to fly around in the dark."

"Mmh, it could be quite dangerous to approach them. And they are very good at hiding. We'll have to be careful they don't sneak up on us first," responded Firth.

Cautiously they weaved their way between the trees, always trying not to expose themselves to the nightly predators, who might mistake them for small birds or dragonflies. Suddenly, a large shadow swept over their heads, its tailwind swirling them around. Firth saw its sharp claws reaching out for them.

"Quick Ardeen, it's an owl!" he shouted.

They dived back into the tree branches to take

shelter among the leaves.

"That was a close call," panted Ardeen, "do you think it's gone?"

"I'm not sure," responded Firth, listening into the darkness. "Owls hardly make any noise when they're flying."

They carefully peeked out from behind the leaf they had chosen as cover. Everything was quiet apart from the usual night sounds of the forest.

"What are we going to do now? We can't spent all night hiding here. We'll never make it to the Magic Rowan Tree in time!" said Ardeen anxiously.

Firth thought for a moment.

"I could try calling it."

"What? So it's easier for it to find its first snack of the night?" exclaimed Ardeen alarmed.

"Granted, it's risky, but it might be willing to help us. We both knew it was going to be a dangerous journey, and it was your risk-taking that got us here in the first place," responded Firth.

"You're right, I'm sorry. It's our best chance," Ardeen said, humbled by his friend's unusually confident response.

"I'm sure it's still nearby. It won't give up so easily on a tasty treat," said Firth. Then he called out to the owl in its own language:

"Owl of the night forest. I am Firth of the

Woodland Fairies. I have come to request your help on an urgent matter. The safety and future of our people depend on it."

Silence followed.

Then, all of a sudden, a beautiful tawny owl landed on the branch right in front of them. Ardeen was about to fly away, when Firth gave him a sign to stand his ground.

"So, Firth of the Woodland Fairies. You require my help? What is it that threatens the fairy folk of the woods?" hooted the owl. Ardeen's knowledge of animal languages was quite limited compared to his friend's. He had no idea how the conversation was going and could only watch and wait patiently.

"Our Magic Sceptre has been destroyed. We need to get to the Magic Rowan Tree in the northern-most forest to be able to make a new one. But it has to be done before the full moon is in its highest point."

"You don't have much time, young fairy friend. It is still a long way to the Magic Rowan Tree, even for a swift flyer like me. But the Woodland Fairies have always been good to us woodland animals and I'll do what I can to help you," offered the owl.

"Could you carry us further north through the night? It is too dangerous for us to fly in the dark. We might get mistaken for food," Firth added with a wink.

"I will carry you until the sun rises. Then I will have to find some food for myself. Who is your friend? He's a quiet fellow. I like that," said the owl.

"This is my friend, Ardeen. He's apprentice to our guardian of the Magic Sceptre, Ealdwode. He's very well versed in spells, but not so much in the language of animals," responded Firth.

"Well then, Firth of the Woodland Fairies, and Ardeen, apprentice to the guardian of the Magic Sceptre, climb on, we have a long journey ahead. My name is Kowen."

Firth and Ardeen settled themselves in the feathery plume on Kowen's back. As soon as they were comfortable, Kowen spread his majestic wings and plunged himself into the darkness.

Firth filled Ardeen in on the conversation with their new friend over a bite to eat. Neither of them had eaten since they'd left in the morning, and Ardeen was beginning to feel faint. Soon afterwards, he fell into an exhausted sleep, while Firth stayed awake a bit longer to chat with Kowen.

"Tell me, Firth," the owl asked. "How did the Magic Sceptre come to be broken? I have roamed this forest for a long time and have heard a great many stories about the Woodland Fairies, but I've never heard of the sceptre being broken."

"Well, it has been broken before, I believe. But

that was a very long time ago. Unfortunately it was my friend here, who broke the sceptre, but it was an accident. He was trying to heal his mother, who's very ill," explained Firth.

"Worry for our loved ones can make us blind to the risks and dangers that come with fear."

Firth fell silent and pondered over the wise words of the owl and soon fell asleep himself.

Ardeen and Firth had an abrupt awakening in the early hours of the morning, when Kowen suddenly landed on a branch. It was still dark, but a faint pink glow in the distance to their right promised daylight was near.

"I'm afraid I'll have to leave you now. I need to find some food before the sunlight ruins my hunt. The Magic Rowan Tree is not far away now. You should reach it within the next couple of hours. Just keep flying north. Farewell my fairy friends."

And before either of them could even thank him, Kowen had taken flight and disappeared into the shadows below.

Still drowsy, the fairy boys looked around to find their bearings. The forest up north was much older and denser than in their part of the forest. The trees were much taller and seemed to be even more ancient than their old oak tree. It also felt much wilder, much more dangerous. Warily, they continued their journey on their own now, weaving in and out of thick branches which were sometimes so interwoven, that it was hard to tell which tree they belonged to.

Ardeen and Firth were both very quiet during this part of their journey. Firstly, because they really had to concentrate where they were going and to keep flying in the right direction. But there was also a strange feeling that had overcome them. Not quite malicious, but also not entirely friendly. They thought it best to make as little noise as possible and get to the Magic Rowan Tree as quickly as they could.

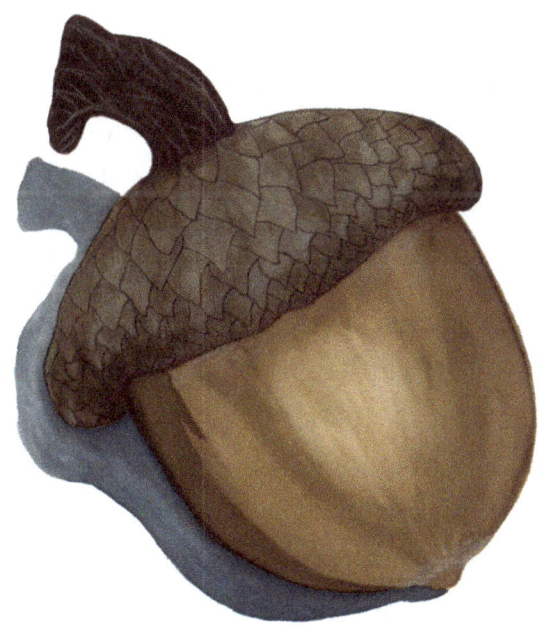

THE MAGIC ROWAN TREE

A couple of hours later, just as Kowen had told them, they indeed arrived at a clearing in which stood the most majestic rowan tree either of them had ever seen. Golden sunlight illuminated the clearing. But the rowan tree emitted a glow from the inside as well. It was surrounded by a brilliant aura of gold shimmering light, gently pulsating with the energy of its magic.

Ardeen was excited to have found the Magic Rowan Tree and rushed towards it to begin his search for the perfect twigs, but as soon as he reached the tree, he found that he couldn't get passed the field of magic surrounding it.

"What's wrong?" Firth enquired, who had approached the tree a bit more cautiously.

"I can't seem to fly any closer to the tree to pick the twigs," responded Ardeen. "Let's approach on foot. Maybe its magic won't let anything fly close to it." But just as he said it, a little nightingale flew straight past them into the tree, and settled on a branch.

"Okay, that's not it then, I guess. But why won't

it let us through?" Ardeen asked rather frustrated. That's just what he needed, he thought. Any delay in getting the twigs would put his mother's life at risk.

"I think we might have to ask its permission," suggested Firth.

Ardeen followed Firth reluctantly to the ground to find a safe and quiet place to sit. They settled into the long grass near the rowan tree.

"I think it needs to be you who talks to it," said Firth. "I will keep watch so you're undisturbed."

Firth was probably right in what he suggested, Ardeen thought. But his tiredness and frustration, additionally fuelled by their lack of time, made it next to impossible for Ardeen to focus. Nevertheless, he sat down and closed his eyes. He took a few deep breaths and tried to establish a connection with the Magic Rowan Tree. His mind was flooded with images of his sick mother lying in her hammock, the look of shock and despair on his father's and sister's face, when they found out he'd performed the ritual, Ealdwode's look of disappointment when he saw the broken sceptre and realisation that his apprentice had disobeyed him yet again.

"It's no use," Ardeen snapped jumping up. "I can't do it. I just can't concentrate."

Firth grabbed Ardeen's arm to make him look into his eyes.

"Ardeen, there is no other way and you know it."

"But..."

"I have stood by you in every reckless experiment you wanted to try, when you didn't heed danger, and I am here with you now, as you feel scared, angry and frustrated. But this time, you have to clean up your mess yourself. Find your focus and speak to the rowan tree, or have you learned nothing from your mistakes? I know you can do it. For your mother's sake."

Ardeen was quite shocked to hear his friend talk to him so firmly, and quite frankly, Firth was very much surprised by it himself. It was, however, exactly what Ardeen needed to hear. He only nodded and sat back down. This time, as the images again started to flood his mind, he allowed to forgive himself for his mistake, let his anger and frustration ebb away, and became grateful for the love and friendship he was surrounded by, and the experiences he had been allowed to have. Finally reaching a place of calm, he saw a light in front of his eyes, and a faint voice whispered through the glow.

"Ardeen of the Woodland Fairies, you have blatantly ignored the rules of Woodland Magic. You have jeopardised your mother's life and the future of all Woodland Fairies, because you didn't trust in the ancient magic of the woodlands. Tell me, why would you deserve another chance?" The voice sounded young and ancient at the same time. Ardeen couldn't make out if it was a male or female voice, and though the words were hard, he didn't feel afraid.

"I know I have let everyone down, and I am really sorry. I was scared it would be too late for my mother if I waited any longer," Ardeen responded.

"Fear doesn't achieve anything. You were reckless. Not because you were bold, but because you were scared. Fear fogs up the brain and doesn't let you see beyond the immediate reality. As the future guardian of the Magic Sceptre, you should have known better."

"I understand that now, and I promise that I won't let fear stand in my way again or make me question our magic."

Then, there was silence. The light was still there, but the voice didn't speak to him for several minutes. Ardeen waited patiently and calmly as he felt this was a test he had to pass.

"Very well, then," said the voice finally. "I hope you have learned your lesson. You may come and choose the twigs for a new Magic Sceptre."

"Thank you, thank you very much," said Ardeen relieved.

Ardeen jumped up so quickly, crying "I've done

it!" that it gave Firth quite a shock.

"Let's go, Firth," he called in great excitement. "I have the permission of the Magic Rowan Tree to pick what we need!"

Not even awaiting Firth's response, he rushed towards the magic tree and passed through the magic barrier as if it didn't exist. Firth, however, noticed that he could not.

"Ardeen, I can't get through," he shouted over to his friend, whom he hadn't seen so exhilarated in a long time.

Ardeen came back to him, his mood slightly dampened.

"I guess it is my task and mine alone to select the perfect branches and proof myself worthy of our magic. Wait here for me, I've got this."

Ardeen flew several times around the tree, then weaved through the branches like a tiny weaving shuttle, all the while reciting the precise instructions he had received from Ealdwode. He knew time was pressing, but this time, he would get it right, he would take his time and only choose the absolute perfect twigs for the new sceptre. It took him several hours, but in the end, he had indeed found all the twigs that matched Ealdwode's specifications exactly. Finally satisfied, he returned to Firth and together they began their long flight back home.

HOMEWARD BOUND

Not long into their journey, Firth heard the song of a redstart and called to it in it's own language. After explaining the situation, the pretty bird by the name of Reed, called to his mate, Blaze, and agreed to carry the two fairy boys as long as they could. They made good progress, when Ardeen noticed a shadow above them. It was hard to tell what it was, as the forest was still very thick and the tree tops often blocked the view of the sky.

"Firth, I believe we're being followed," he said, pointing to the sky.

Firth looked up. At first he couldn't see anything, but then realised that the shadow was a red kite.

"Quick, we need to find some shelter," he cried. But it was too late. While Firth and Ardeen had been scanning the sky above them, Reed and Blaze were heading towards a clearing in the wood and

came out into the open just as Firth was shouting his warning. The kite saw its chance and swooped down towards the two redstarts.

"We have to get off, otherwise they won't stand a chance against the kite," cried Firth, already letting go and racing towards safety at the edge of the clearing. Ardeen did the same just moments later, but lost his balance and nearly dropped all the precious twigs. He heard frantic flapping of wings all around him, but could only focus on getting to safety himself. Reaching Firth he panted, "did they make it?"

"Yes, they did. They were so amazing. They confused the kite by flying off in different directions. Brave little birds. But I'm afraid we've lost our transport now, and we couldn't even thank them."

"I nearly dropped the twigs as well. Reed and Blaze have brought us a long way, but we must make haste. Let's go," responded Ardeen.

Now that they were on their way home, Ardeen couldn't help but wonder how his mother was doing. Had the half-finished ritual given her more time, or was it already too late for her healing? He felt panic rising in him, but reminded himself of what the Magic Rowan Tree had told him. I trust in our magic and believe that everything is just as it should be, he thought. Feeling reassured, he pressed on.

At nightfall, Firth convinced a little owl to help them. It was great to be able to rest their wings, but neither of them could think of falling asleep. They spent the night in almost complete silence and wide awake. Firth noticed a change in his friend. He was no longer a young fairy boy, experimenting with spells without worrying about the consequences, but appeared older to him, calmer and more mature, with an aura of inner certainty.

At daylight, they thanked the little owl and bid it farewell. It wouldn't be too long now before they were back home, and both were anxious to know what would await them there. A couple of hours later, their surroundings started to look familiar. The cave, where they had picked the goblin gold moss for their magic fire spell, was not far from here. How long ago all of this felt. The vicinity to their home and families gave them additional speed and by noon they arrived back at Ardeen's home.

Ardeen stopped at the entrance to their home. He was nervous to enter, scared of what he might find there. But as always, Firth was at his side.

"I'm sure your mother is alright and waiting for your return. Either way, I'm here for you."

"Thank you, Firth. I couldn't have done this without you," Ardeen responded. Quietly they entered. Ardeen immediately saw his father, sister and Ealdwode surrounding his parents' hammock.

"Is she…?" he couldn't finish the sentence.

Hearing his voice, they all looked towards him, and Sylvan and Pherenice rushed over to greet him.

"She's weak, but now that you're back, I'm sure she'll be alright," his father reassured him.

Ealdwode had also flown down to him, visibly relieved at his return.

"My boy, you're back. And you, too, Firth. Have you found the tree?" he enquired.

"Yes, we have, and here are the twigs," said Ardeen, handing the twigs to Ealdwode.

"Oh no, you keep hold of those. You have done well, Ardeen, and I'm so sorry that I cannot allow you to rest just yet. You have a new sceptre to build." Turning to Firth, he continued:

"Firth, loyal, brave, Firth. Go home and get some rest and be with your family. They have missed you dearly. But do come back before midnight. You have more than earned the right to be part of the ritual tonight." With a nod to Sylvan, he turned to leave. Ardeen hugged his friend tightly.

"Thank you. For everything," he whispered into his ear. Giving his father and sister a final hug he, too, turned to follow Ealdwode to the Old Oak.

THE NEW MAGIC SCEPTRE

Ardeen looked forward to the familiarity of the Old Oak. The last few days had been so strange and frightening, that being surrounded by all the scrolls again was like a comfort blanket. As soon as he entered, he felt different than expected though. The Old Oak felt different, and it looked different too. Everything inside it shimmered with a subtle golden glow. Every scroll, jar and bowl, even the oak itself emitted the most beautiful light he'd ever seen. It was even more divine than dappled light falling through the trees on a misty morning. Ardeen looked around open mouthed.

"Aha, you can see it now," said Ealdwode, when he noticed the look on his apprentice's face.

"What is this, Ealdwode? What has happened to the Old Oak?"

"It has always looked like this, at least to us guardians. It seems you have brought back more than a few twigs from the Magic Rowan Tree. You are finally ready."

"Ready for what?"

"To be a guardian of the Woodland Fairies and our Magic Sceptre, of course!" exclaimed Ealdwode with a smile. "But there's no time to celebrate at the moment. You have a sceptre to make."

Ealdwode had already prepared all the ingredients for the healing ritual, so all they needed to do, was to build the sceptre.

"As you were the one who broke the old sceptre, and as future guardian of the new sceptre, you will have to design the new sceptre on your own. Think about what it stands for, and what it means to the Woodland Fairies, and to you. It will serve you best if you are truly connected to it," explained Ealdwode.

"But we're running out of time, and I'm not sure I can think straight after this journey. It will take me too long," cried Ardeen. "Please, you must help me, Ealdwode."

"You have learned to trust our magic, Ardeen. Now let it guide you."

With that, Ealdwode withdrew to another corner of the Old Oak, and left Ardeen alone with the twigs of the Magic Rowan Tree and the gemstone spread out in front of him. Ardeen closed his eyes and took a few deep breaths.

What does it stand for? he asked himself. The Magic Sceptre represents our traditions, our history and heritage, but also our duty. For the Woodland Fairies, it is the source of our magic, and a symbol that what we do is important and right. And to me? To me, it means unwavering trust in our magic, in nature's magic, a connection to everlasting truth, a bond that is both flexible and strong.

Opening his eyes he looked down at the pieces in front of him, and realised that they had all these qualities. Some of the twigs were old and gnarly, but strong and unbreakable. Others where thin, but flexible and bendy. And they all came from the most ancient tree he had ever seen, which renewed itself every spring.

His hands started working. To Ardeen it felt like he was only half conscious in the process, but just let it happen. With nimble fingers, he weaved and inter-twined the twigs, forming a cup to hold the gemstone securely in the middle. He inspected the sceptre carefully before putting the gemstone back to where it belonged, and decided that something was missing. Rushing around the Old Oak he found the feathers of the birds that had helped him and Firth complete their journey to and from the Magic Rowan Tree on time — a tawny owl feather, a robin feather, a little owl feather, and the feather of a redstart — and tied them to the sceptre. Then he carefully placed the gemstone in it.

The Old Oak filled with the warm red glow of the gemstone. Ealdwode looked up from the scrolls he'd been reading.

"You did it, Ardeen!" he exclaimed joyfully, and rushed over to him. "My dear boy, you did it!"

"It's so beautiful," whispered Ardeen, almost lost for words.

"It is time to heal your mother," Ealdwode whispered back.

MAGNA LUNA

Ardeen and Ealdwode picked up the Magic Sceptre and bundle with the healing powder, which Ealdwode had already prepared, and set-off to Ardeen's home. The moon was high in the sky and looked larger than Ardeen had ever seen it.

Firth was already there, and his mother sat upright in the hammock, ready for the ritual. She was weak, but had found strength in the knowledge that her son had returned safely with the material to build a new Magic Sceptre. Ardeen rushed over to her, hardly able to contain his tears.

"Ardeen, hold the sceptre out into the moonlight, the moon is nearly at its peak," Ealdwode told him.

He held the sceptre out of a small opening as before and let the moonlight surround the sceptre. As the silver light touched the sceptre, it began to sparkle and glow. This time not in red, but with a cool, silver glow. It was wonderful to behold.

In the meantime, Ealdwode had prepared the

paste with Firth's help.

"This should do," he said, and called Ardeen back over to them.

Everyone was silent and looked tensely towards the sceptre. When they saw its beauty and silvery glow, their tension melted away, and made room for excitement and hope.

With a nod from Ealdwode, both him and Ardeen began to chant the spell, while Ealdwode applied the paste and Ardeen held the sceptre over the wound. For a moment, nothing happened, but then the sceptre began to glow even brighter, this time in both silver moonlight and deep red. The light ignited the paste on Nemorosa's wound and seemed to burn the poison within her. Nemorosa experienced an extreme, but not painful, tingling sensation as the blue line, that had crept really close to her heart by now, withdrew further and further, until all that was left was a pale scar where the badger had scratched her.

For a few minutes, no one spoke and stared open mouthed at the former nasty wound.

"It worked." Ardeen was the first to speak. "It really worked!"

Then they all broke out into joyous laughter. Many happy tears were shed and heartfelt hugs exchanged.

"I am so proud of you, Ardeen," said his mother.

"You will be an amazing guardian."

"To that, I agree," seconded Ealdwode. "You have truly proven yourself. From now on, the new sceptre will serve you better than me. And although I still have a few years left as official guardian, it will be mainly your duty now to protect our magic, our heritage and the woodlands with everything in them."

"Thank you, but I could not have done it without your trust in me, and especially not without the help of the best friend anyone could ever wish for. Thank you Firth. From now on, I'll be a better friend to you."

And he was. After Nemorosa's complete recovery, and a good rest, Ardeen took over more and more responsibilities as guardian of the Woodland Fairies. Every now and then, he would add a special token to the sceptre. Something, that had meaning to him and reminded him of all the adventures he had, and it made the sceptre stronger than it had ever been before. Nothing could break his bond of trust in nature's magic.

THE END

Other titles in the series:

"This book is a magical read that will captivate your child with its page-turning adventures!"

Louise Jane (CEO The Golden Wizard Book Prize)

FREE colouring templates available from:
https://www.inesholmes.com/downloads

ABOUT THE AUTHOR

 Ines Holmes is a UK-based German writer, author of the 'Magical Tales from Fairyland' series, and two-times winner of The Golden Wizard Book Prize.

The idea for the series sparked from living in the beautiful countryside in the Southwest of England. "There are just so many hidden paths, enchanted forests and magical sunrises /sunsets here, that my imagination can run wild. It's truly magical."

Despite being a German native speaker, Holmes prefers to write in English and then translates the finished work into German. All illustrations are drawn by herself as well.

AN UNFORTUNATE EVENT

The sun rose gently over the late summer meadow. Most flowers were still in a deep slumber with their petals wrapped tightly around them. But in just a few hours, the meadow would be transformed from a sea of sparkling dew-drops to an ocean bursting with colour and vibrating with the buzzing of bees, the fluttering of butterflies and the crickety-crick of grasshoppers and other insects.

A ray of sun tickled Starflower's nose. She stretched her slender arms and legs, while shaking the morning dew off her wings. Her body was a translucent shade of pale pinks and blues, flowing through her like misty clouds. Starflower had spent the night sleeping on the leaf of a foxglove. Her mother, Meliantha, and father, Trillium, were sleeping on the leaf next to her.

Starflower and her parents are Meadow Fairies. These are small and delicate creatures, no bigger than a large butterfly. They have crystalline, shimmering bodies and wings, reflecting the colour of the sky and flowers around them – ever changing and always partly invisible, like a brilliant reflection of light on rippling water. They can also become invisible at will or change only the colour of their wings, to look like butterflies, which makes them incredibly difficult to spy.

"It's such a fine morning, Mother," said Starflower, "can I go and play with Sundrop? Please, Mother, can I?" Meadow Fairies of all ages love to play, but especially the younger ones.

"Of course you can," responded her mother, "but be back soon. We have to collect some nectar today. Summer is coming to an end and we need to make sure we gather enough nectar and honeydew for the colder months."

"I will, Mother. See you later," cried Starflower, who was already on her way to find her best friend Sundrop.

Meadow Fairy families live scattered across the entire meadow and change their sleeping places every night to avoid detection, but families that know each other well tend to stay fairly close together. Therefore, it didn't take Starflower very long to find Sundrop and her family.

Sundrop enjoyed watching the sunrise and warming-up her wings in the sun while having a sip of fresh morning dew, unlike her friend Starflower, who was always out and about as soon as the sun stretched her first pale rays of light across the meadow.

"Good morning, Starflower," called Sundrop. She had already seen Starflower fluttering towards her. "You are up early…as usual," she added with a laugh that rang like crystal bells.

"Good morning!" Starflower smiled at her friend and her family. "Nothing like a refreshing flight through the morning mist! Let's go, Sundrop. I've seen some wonderful spider webs on the way here."

"Oh, that sounds amazing! Can I go, Mum, Dad?"

"Off you go," said her father, Vervain, "but be sure to be back in time to collect nectar, you two!"

"We will." The girls laughed in unison and fluttered away like dancing specks of light.

Now, you might wonder *What's so great about sticky spider webs?* You see, for a Meadow Fairy, a spider web full of delicate drops of morning dew is a most exciting thing. If the morning sun shines on it at just the right angle, it creates a wonderful spectre of smaller and bigger rainbows, which is not only beautiful to behold, but also an amazing playground. Meadow Fairies can slide down such rainbows just like human children can on slides in the park. The really big rain-bows you can see across the sky can only be used by leprechauns, of course.

Starflower and Sundrop were in luck. Even from a distance they could see the kaleidoscopic dance of the rainbows shimmering on the spider webs. Down they slid first one rainbow, then another, and another, until they were out of breath, and laughing with delight.

"Oh, be careful!" Sundrop called out to Starflower, who nearly caught her wings in the web as she was rushing to the next rainbow. Fortunately, she managed to change direction just in time. Meadow Fairies might be immortal, but they can still get injured, especially on their fragile wings.

Soon, though, there were not enough dew-drops left, and the sun had risen higher in the sky. The little fairy girls had now taken on the colour of a hazy yellow, with bright clouds of blue, violet, red and pink rushing through them as they fluttered past the colourful meadow flowers, which were slowly opening their faces to the warm morning sun.

"Let's play Bouncy Petal," cried Sundrop, and they flew from one flower to the next, bouncing on each blossom, shaking off the last of the dew-drops and giggling all the way. A particularly large drop landed on a grasshopper underneath. He didn't look too pleased about this as he wiped the water off his wings.

"I'm so sorry," called Starflower over her shoulder, but she was already too far away for the grasshopper to hear. They finally sat down on a large purple blossom of a monkshood plant and looked across the meadow.

"I guess it will be autumn soon," said Sundrop.

"Many flowers are losing their petals, and the grasses have turned more yellow than the bright, fresh green they used to be."

"You're right. The nights are getting colder now as

well, and the days are so much shorter and don't warm up so much anymore. I guess we better get back and help our parents with the nectar."

Meadow Fairies don't store any food or drink over the spring and summer. There are plenty of flowers for everyone to drink from, and all of them taste differently. Some are really sweet and others have a sour or bitter aftertaste, and some even sting a little bit on the tongue. The fairies also drink the fresh morning dew from the petals and leaves. For a special treat, they ask the bees for some meadow honey or they make spicy mead from the tiny seeds of meadow grasses. Towards the end of summer, however, Meadow Fairies start to store nectar for the cooler months, when the flowers have lost their blossoms and the meadow is slowly dying, just to return with renewed strength and colour the next year. During this time, they go into hibernation until spring, as they don't care for the cold and wet weather. As soon as the last meadow flowers have died off, they join the Stone Fairies, who live in dry stone walls alongside fields and forests. They spend a few weeks in each other's company, exchanging stories and wisdom from the elders, and celebrating their short union, until November Eve, when the Meadow Fairies withdraw to the most concealed and protected holes in the wall to hibernate. The Stone Fairies watch over them and enjoy the nectar and honeydew the Meadow

Fairies have brought with them, always keeping some in spare for the Meadow Fairies to drink when they wake up again. It gives them strength for their journey back to their meadows.

Starflower and Sundrop found their parents, who were already busy collecting nectar from the flowers that were still in bloom.

"There you are!" called Meliantha. "We thought you had forgotten all about your chores today."

There was a twinkling in her eyes and a smile on her lips. She had never been able to seriously be cross with her daughter. Who didn't enjoy a bit of fun and play?

"We have already filled these corncockle blossoms," said Sundrop's mother, Merrybell, pointing at a number of funnel-shaped blossoms, neatly tied up with blades of meadow grass. "Can you take them to the burrow, please? But do be careful not to drop them!"

"Don't worry, Mother, we will be careful," said Sundrop, and both girls picked up a blossom and fluttered off to the burrow.

Meadow Fairies find an empty rabbit burrow or tunnel left behind by moles, rats or mice to gather together their food for the winter.

The closer the fairy girls got to the burrow, the busier the meadow got. Fairies fluttered towards it from all directions of the meadow, all now shimmering brightly in the midday sun. Everyone was so busy, Starflower and Sundrop had to wait a good while just to drop their blossoms off. Once they had entered the burrow, they were awestruck by the amount of nectar-filled blossoms around them.

"Look!" exclaimed Starflower. "The blossoms are stacked right up to the ceiling. And it smells so good… yummy! It's making me really hungry. Let's go and find some nectar for ourselves."

"But we have to make at least two more trips just to drop off the blossoms our parents have already filled. We can't just let them lie there."

"Alright, alright. Let's go then, but after that we eat and play Seek the Fairy."

"Alright," giggled Sundrop.

But there were so many blossoms to take to the burrow now that the girls didn't have any time to play that day, nor the next one, or the day after that. The days were quickly getting shorter, colder and windier, and the fairies were all busy with the final preparations before they would join the Stone Fairies.

This is no fun at all, thought Starflower to herself one morning. *I don't want to spend the last days of summer carrying nectar to the burrow. Surely it won't hurt if I go out to play for a bit? Just a couple of hours?*

The morning was cool, and dark clouds were massing in the sky. It would be raining soon, but that didn't stop Starflower. Off she fluttered across the meadow looking for a little adventure.

I'll go and find Sundrop first, she thought. *I'm sure she'd love to come as well.*

She soon found Sundrop busy at work helping her parents. Sundrop was just about to set off with another petal filled with delicious nectar. Starflower followed her at a distance until they were out of her parent's sight, then quickly caught up with her.

"Hallo, Sundrop! Let's have a race."

"Huh? Oh, it's you!" said Sundrop. "Shouldn't you be helping your parents?"

"Yes, I know, but the last few days have been so dull, and this will probably be our last chance before we go into hibernation."

"I know, Starflower, but I really have to bring this blossom to the burrow," said Sundrop, although she was as keen as Starflower to have a bit of fun.

"You can hide it here and we'll take it to the burrow together later. We'll only be gone for a little while. Please, Sundrop," pleaded Starflower.

"Alright then, but only for a little bit."

They hid the blossom and fluttered away. Both fairy girls loved to race across the meadow, brushing past the flowers and grasses that were now bent down by the wind. Soon, it also started to rain, but still they flew faster and faster until...

"Oh, help!"

A strong gush of wind had picked Sundrop up and blown her sideways into the hooked burs of a burdock plant! Her wings got pinned to the plant as the spiky burs tore into them.

"Sundrop!" gasped Starflower. She turned around and flew back to help her friend.

"Don't come too close, Starflower, or the same

might happen to you."

"Can you free your wings?"

Sundrop wriggled around trying to release her wings from the hooks, but that only made it worse.

"I'm stuck! You have to get help, Starflower."

"This is all my fault. I should never have convinced you to come with me!" cried Starflower.

"It was my own choice, but you have to get my parents. Be quick! Every gush of wind is pushing the burs deeper into my wings."

"I'll be as quick as I can!" Starflower rushed back to get help, while poor Sundrop was pinned to the burs swaying in the wind. Luckily, fairies don't experience pain the same way as humans do, otherwise this would have been a very excruciating experience for little Sundrop.

In the meantime, both their parents were getting uneasy. They had suspected that their daughters had snuck off to enjoy a few moments of freedom before winter, but the children had been gone a while now, and it was not like them to neglect their duties for so long.

"I'm worried something might have happened to our dear child," Meliantha said to Trillium.

"You worry too much, Meliantha. Starflower is a bright little fairy, she can look after herself."

"I know, but still. I'd rather we went looking for her. Let's find Merrybell and Vervain. Maybe she's flown over there to play with Sundrop."

They soon found them collecting nectar from some columbines nearby.

"Hello, Merrybell. Have you seen Starflower?"

"No, I'm afraid I haven't," said Merrybell. "But Sundrop also hasn't returned from her trip to the burrow yet. They have probably gone to play a bit. Though it has been a while now, I have to say, and the weather is turning nasty."

"We should go looking for them. I'm worried something might have happened," said Meliantha.

"But where shall we start?" asked Trillium. "The meadow is huge, and what if they come back in the meantime?"

Just as Meliantha was about to respond, she saw her daughter rushing towards them in great haste. She was completely out of breath as she landed on the leaf next to her mother.

"Where is Sundrop?" cried Merrybell.

"Wind…hooks…burs…can't…free herself," panted Starflower.

"Catch your breath, child, and then tell us what happened," said Meliantha, trying to soothe her daughter.

Collecting herself, Starflower explained what had

happened a little more slowly.

"I'm so sorry," she sobbed.

"Come, Starflower, can you show us the way? We have to free Sundrop as soon as we can," said Vervain.

They all set off together. The weather was getting worse. Black clouds were coming in and the wind whistled across the meadow.

And how had poor Sundrop fared during all this time? She had been desperately trying to free herself, but only damaged her wings even more. The strong wind kept pressing her into the hooks of the bur. She was now trying to stay as still as possible, hoping that Starflower would soon return with her parents, but it was getting dark quickly. Suddenly, she saw a group of sparkling lights in the last light of the day, coming straight towards her.

"I'm over here!" Sundrop shouted as loudly as she could. They had found her.

"Oh my dear, poor child. We'll get you out of there."

"We can't get too close, otherwise we'll get blown into the burs as well," said Vervain. "We have to find a flower stem or stick that we can use to free Sundrop's wings."

He and Trillium returned in just a few minutes. In the meantime, Meliantha had taken a better look at the damage to Sundrop's wings, while Merrybell tried to comfort her daughter.

"I'm afraid she won't be able to fly once her wings are free, they are too badly injured," said Meliantha.

"We will have to catch her when she falls, then," Vervain responded. "Trillium and I will free up her wings with the flower stems and you two catch her," said Vervain. They cautiously set to work while Merrybell and Meliantha hovered underneath Sundrop, cautious not to be blown into the burs themselves.

"Not long now, my darling. Don't worry, we will catch you," said Merrybell.

It was very precarious work, but eventually they succeeded in levering Sundrop's wings from the hooks, and she dropped safely into the arms of her mother and Meliantha, who then flew her off to a plant nearby. Merrybell hugged her daughter tightly and Vervain joined the embrace.

Starflower was riddled with guilt.

"She'll be okay," she heard her mother's whisper in her ear, who had landed beside her, giving her hand a squeeze.

"We have to find a safe place to spend the night. It's too dangerous to carry Sundrop in this wind, and it's too dark to see now anyway," said Trillium after a few minutes.

They all passed the night together on the leaves of a

coneflower without any further incidents. Luckily, the next morning dawned brightly and they sat down together over a rich breakfast of sweet nectar that soon revived their energy and spirit. But what was there to be done about Sundrop's torn wings? Meadow Fairies have great self-healing powers, but her wings were too damaged even for that.

"You should consult the queen," said Meliantha. "She'll know what to do."

"Then we better summon her quickly," said Merrybell.